THE
BONE KEEPER

by Megan McDonald ≈ paintings by G. Brian Karas

A DK INK BOOK
DK PUBLISHING, INC.

If you listen to the desert,
if you listen,
you may hear
a laughing,
a chanting,
a singing.

They call her Owl Woman.
They call her Rattlesnake Woman.
They call her Bone Woman.

Bone Woman is old,
older than the Joshua tree.
She is bent and stooped,
closer to earth than sky.
Her hands are withered
like some ancient oracle.
Through a wrinkle on the sole of her foot,
she feels everything.

Some say she has three heads,
past, present, and future.
Some say she carries the snake,
walks with the wild hare.

Some say Bone Woman brings the dead back to life.

She is Hunter.
She is Gatherer.
She is Keeper of the Bones.

Like the desert pack rat,
the harvester ant,
Bone Woman lives deep in a cave,
a cave cluttered with bones, bones.

She walks in death's valley,
where the mammoths once roamed,
the empty quarter,
the place from which there is no return.

By day Bone Woman sifts and searches the sand,
searches and sifts
for bones, bones,
bleached white in the desert sun.

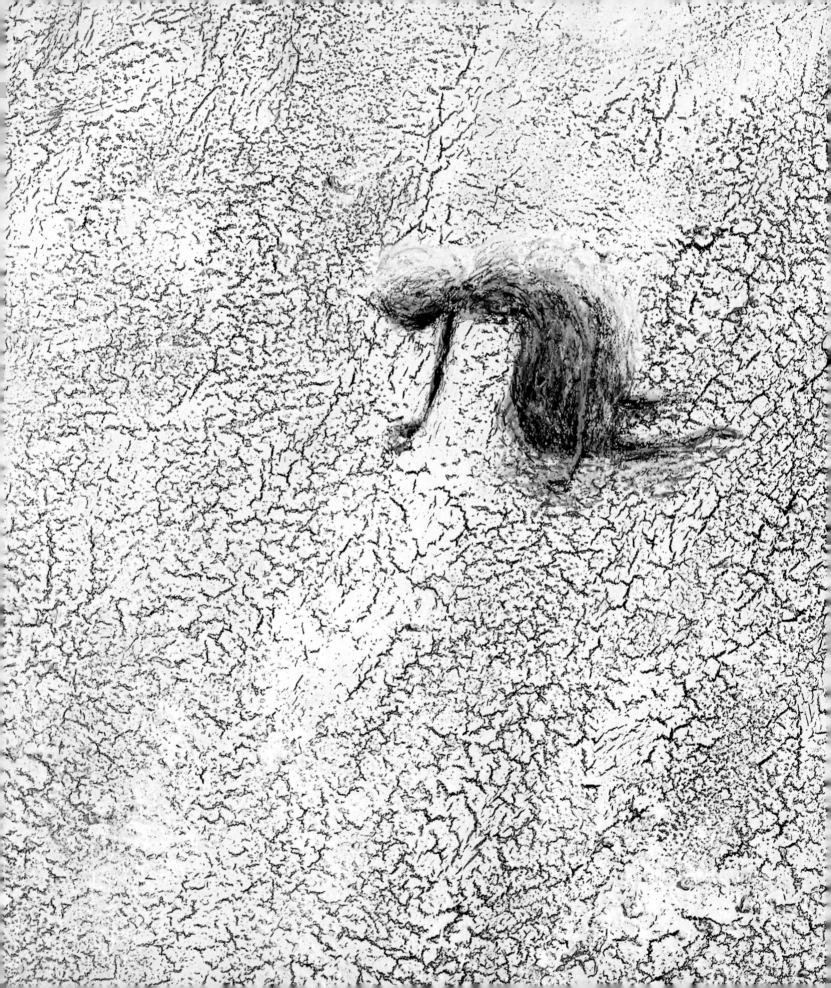

She goes
where the barrel cactus points south,
where the sidewinder leaves its track,
where the vulture flies.

She knows.
She sees things
smaller than a grain of sand.

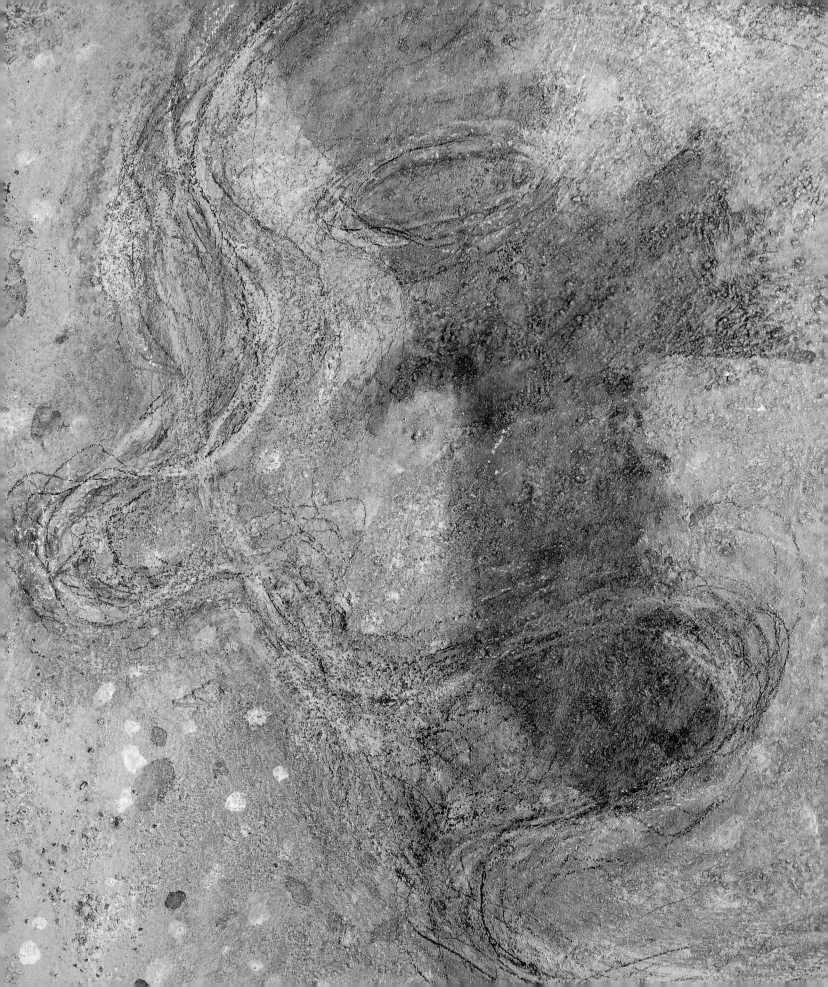

Bones, bones are everywhere
and nowhere.
Wind tosses them across dunes
and bare rock,
into dry washes and arroyos,
the way seeds are scattered
on the sides of hills
waiting years
to become cactus.

Bone Woman sifts through the sand
and the sand beneath the sand.
One by one by one,
she collects
each lonely bone.

By night
Bone Woman
calls to bat and badger,
kit fox and kangaroo rat,
rattlesnake and ring-tailed cat.
They move
among strange rock shapes
when the shadows are just right.

They watch.

Bone Woman
rattles the dry bones, bones,
studies them with her milky eye,
piecing them together,
a puzzle,
a painting.

One by one by one,
spine of snake, skull of lizard.
Bone by bone by bone,
claw of badger,
   wishbone of owl,
      wing bone of bat.
            Skeleton Maker.

At last
every bone is in place
except one—that tiny piece
at the tip of the tip of the tail.

For days
Bone Woman chews on the taproot of the smoke tree,
rubs it on her brow,
pricks her finger
with the needle of the cat claw.

At last it is time.
A dust devil blows and swirls,
a whirlwind of sand.
The final bone is found
at her feet.

Bone Woman
carries the bone home to her cave.
She lights a fire,
then slowly,
carefully
puts the last bone in place,
that tiny tip of the tip of the tail.

Bone Woman
dances with one side of her body,
waits with the other.

She chants over the bones, bones.
Moans.
Her moaning becomes a wail,
her wail, a howl.

It rises and floats
up, up, up into the night,
higher than hawk upon hawk
perched atop the saguaro.
It pierces the night,
sharper than a thousand thorns.

The floor of Bone Woman's cave rumbles.
The bones, bones
begin to move,
shake,
stand.

Muscle, tendon,
and sinew twist.
Heart beats,
lungs swell.
Flesh appears.
The ghost creature
grows fur,
black and gray
and white.

Eyes blink.
Jaw snaps.
Tail twitches.
Yellow eyes stare.

A wolf!

The wolf stretches,
springs to life,
leaps from the cave,
lopes across the desert sand,
howling deep into the night.

They say
if you listen to the desert,
if you listen,
you may hear
a laughing,
a chanting,
a singing.

Some say it is Bone Woman,
Skeleton Maker,
Keeper of the Bones.

Some say
if you wander in the desert
when the shadows are just right,
you may see a flash
of black and gray and white hair.

It is the mystery of the bones.

Some say you may hear a howling,
far and away, deep into the night

and not know
if it is wolf or woman,
woman or wolf.

For Pauline—M.M.

With special thanks to the Phoenix Public Library
and the Heard Museum—B.K.

A Richard Jackson Book

Ink

DK Publishing, Inc.
95 Madison Avenue
New York, New York 10016

Visit us on the World Wide Web at http://www.dk.com

Library of Congress Cataloging-in-Publication Data
McDonald, Megan.
The bone keeper / by Megan McDonald; illustrated by G. Brian Karas.
p.   cm.
"A Richard Jackson book."
Summary: The Bone Woman searches the desert gathering bones
to create a wondrous creature.
ISBN 0-7894-2559-9
[1. Deserts—Fiction.   2. Bones—Fiction.   3. Wolves—Fiction.]
I. Karas, G. Brian, ill.   II. Title.
PZ7.M478419Bo   1998   [E]—dc21   98-3680   CIP   AC

The illustrations for this book were prepared
with a variety of materials, conventional and otherwise.
The text of this book is set in 18 point Aldus.
Printed and bound in U.S.A.

First Edition, 1999
10   9   8   7   6   5   4   3   2   1